Fiesta!

by Beatriz McConnie Zapater

Illustrated by
José Ortega

MULTICULTURAL CELEBRATIONS

MODERN CURRICULUM PRESS

Multicultural Celebrations was created under the auspices of
 The Children's Museum, Boston.
Leslie Swartz, Director of Teacher Services,
organized and directed this project with
funding from The Hitachi Foundation.

This story was written in consultation with Inés Maturana
who comes from Colombia.

Design: Gary Fujiwara
Photographs: *5*, Dana Hyde; *6*, Ric Ergenbright;
14, Louis Martin.

 MODERN CURRICULUM PRESS, INC.
13900 Prospect Road
Cleveland, Ohio 44136

ISBN 0-8136-2280-8 (soft cover)   0-8136-2281-6 (hard cover)
4 5 6 7 8 9 10   95 94 93
Simon & Schuster   A Paramount Communications Company

Chucho's father came home from work very excited.

"Chucho, where is everyone? I have some news!"

"María! Mami! Papi's home and he's got
something to tell us," yelled Chucho as he climbed
from the arm to the back of the couch.

"M'ijo! How many times do I have to tell you not to climb on the back of the couch?" scolded his mother, rushing into the living room.

María laughed, "Sometimes, little brother, I think you are *un chivo*—part mountain goat."

"Listen everyone," Papi said. "My friend Tito has asked us all to go with him to the Fiesta de Santiago next Saturday."

"A fiesta like the ones we had in Colombia?" asked María.

"I don't remember any fiestas in Colombia. I don't even remember Colombia," Chucho interrupted.

"Well," said Mami, "you were just three years old when we came to the States. But we have told you many things about our country."

"Yes, but I wish I could see the country where I was born for myself," Chucho said. "Couldn't we go there for a visit?"

"Maybe . . . maybe, Chucho. A trip like that costs much money—*mucha plata*," Chucho's father explained.

"Papi, tell us about the fiesta! Isn't Tito from Guatemala?" asked María. "Is his fiesta the same as ours?"

"Almost every town in Latin America has its own fiesta—all named for different saints. There are Fiestas de San Pacho, Fiestas de Loíza, and others. Here in the States we get together in the summer to hold a fiesta for all Hispanics, no matter where they are from."

"What will there be to eat?" asked Chucho, getting down to the most important issue.

Papi laughed, "There will be all kinds of food, and a parade, and a contest where you try to climb a greased pole to reach a cash prize!"

"And Papi, don't forget the music, and the *vacas locas*, people wearing those crazy cow masks. I remember that part," María said.

"Oh yes, and we can all take part in the celebration," Papi continued. "Imagine, the Mosquera family *comparsa*. We'll be the best group in the parade."

So, all the next week the Mosquera family was busy getting ready for the fiesta. Mami and María sewed costumes—*trajes típicos*—for everyone to wear. Chucho thought about the prize money and what they could do with it. And Papi disappeared mysteriously into his workshop every evening after dinner.

Chucho was curious. "What are you making, Papi?"

"Wait and see," was all he would say.

At last the big day arrived. The whole family, dressed in their *trajes típicos*, piled into the car— all except Chucho.

"Where is that Chucho? Chucho!" called Papi.

"Up here, Papi," he answered from the branches of a nearby tree.

"Get down. Must you always be climbing? One day you will hurt yourself. Come—we have to hurry."

As soon as they parked the car, they joined the people from the different *barrios* forming the parade. Whole neighborhoods were there.

"Where's Papi?" Chucho asked, suddenly noticing he was gone. "He'll miss the fun!"

"I don't know," his mother answered. "Maybe he's meeting Tito."

Then Chucho heard firecrackers. Almost at once a green-horned monster burst through the crowd and headed straight for him.

"Ay-y-y!" Chucho shouted and he started to run. "*¡Una vaca loca*! A wild cow!"

He noticed no one else was running, so he turned. "Take off your mask, *vaca loca*, and join your family. You're scaring poor Chucho!" he heard his mother say.

Then Chucho saw his smiling father appear from under the mask. "I did a good job in my workshop—Chucho—yes?"

"Oh yes, Papi," Chucho said with relief.

The music started and the parade began to move. In the lead was Tito's band, his *chirimía*. There were many *comparsas* in the street. Men, women, and children danced and sang.

"I'm getting hungry," Chucho finally shouted to his Papi. "When can we eat?" The street was lined with booths selling foods from Puerto Rico, Mexico, Honduras—all over Latin America. Chucho looked for his favorite Colombian foods—*patacones* and *empanadas*—fried *plantains* and turnovers filled with meat and potatoes.

As they strolled from booth to booth eating,
the Mosqueras heard an announcement over the
loudspeaker. It was time for the *palo encebao*,
the greased pole contest.

"What do you have to do to win the money, Papi?"
Chucho asked.

"Just watch," Papi said as he joined the rest of Tito's
team. They looked on as other teams tried but failed
to reach the cash prize at the top of the slippery
pole.

Then it was their turn. The first man on their team
grabbed the pole and a second man climbed on his
shoulders. Then Tito climbed over both of them and
stood hugging the pole. Last came Papi, slowly
climbing over the shoulders of his teammates.
María and Mami and Chucho cheered wildly.

Papi slowly inched his way up, until the prize was almost within his reach. Suddenly he lost his grip and slid back to where he had started. Papi, looking very unhappy, was covered with smelly grease. Then the crowd began to cheer again. Someone was climbing up on Papi's shoulders.
It was Chucho!

Chucho easily got his balance. His added height was just enough. He reached up and quickly snatched the prize money from the top of the pole.

Chucho was the hero of the day.

"Maybe it is good to have *un chivo* around the house," laughed his mother.

"Very lucky for us," said Papi smiling at Chucho. "With our share of the money maybe a visit to Colombia doesn't have to be only a wish after all."

Glossary

barrios (BAR-ryohs) neighborhoods

chirimía (chee-ree-MEE-ah) a group of musicians; a regional term from Colombia where Fiesta de San Pacho is celebrated

un chivo (OON CHEE-voh) a goat

Chucho (CHEW-choh) a boy's nickname; an informal name for "Jesús"

comparsa (kom-PAHR-sah) a group of people wearing the same costumes and performing dances and songs together

empanadas (em-pah-NAH-dahs) turnovers made from flour or corn which are filled with meat and potatoes

fiesta (FYES-tah) a fair or party

Mami (MAH-mee) informal name for mother; Mommy

M'ijo (MEE-hoh) informal way to say "my son"

mucha plata (MOO-chah PLAH-tah) informal way to say "a lot of money"

palo encebao (PAH-loh en-say-BAH-oh) a greased pole

Papi (PAH-pee) informal name for father; Daddy

patacones (pah-tah-COH-nes) fried green plantains, also called tostones

plantains (plan-TAYNS) South American fruit resembling green bananas

trajes típicos (TRAH-hess TEE-pee-kos) traditional costumes

una vaca loca (OON-ah VAH-cah LOH-kah) a crazy cow; a costumed character dressed like a wild or crazy cow

About the Author

Beatriz McConnie Zapater grew up in Ponce, Puerto Rico, in a large, close-knit family. She moved to Boston to attend school. The focus of her life is the Puerto Rican community and her two sons, Fernando and Andrés. She dreams of being a musician and a photographer.

About the Illustrator

Artist **José Ortega** was born in Guayaquil, Ecuador, and came to the United States in 1970. He received a B.F.A. from the School of Visual Arts. His work is exhibited regularly in New York City. Mr. Ortega enjoys travelling and loves Latin-American music and jazz.